BRANDEIS
HILLEL
DAY SCHOOL
ברנדייס חלל

180 NORTH SAN PEDRO RD.
SAN RAFAEL, CALIFORNIA 94903

ב"ה
Nov 2004

The Jewish value we
found in this book

is . . .

Do not lie

Signed : _Arielle_
me

[signature]
parent

Why Cats Chase Mice

A Story of the Twelve Zodiac Signs

Retold and illustrated by
Mina Harada Eimon

To Mom and Dad

© 1993 Story and Illustrations by Mina Harada Eimon

Heian International, Inc.
1815 West 205th Street, Suite 301
Torrance, CA 90501

ISBN: 0-89346-533-X

First Printing 1993
93 94 95 96 97 10 9 8 7 6 5 4 3 2 1

Printed in Singapore

What does a cat do when he sees a mouse? He chases it, of course! Everybody knows that cats and mice do not get along. But does anybody know why?

Believe it or not, there was once a time when cats and mice were very good friends. In fact, back in those days, all animals were friendly with each other.

4

Each month the animals had a festival, and they sang, danced, and played together. The animals were always on their best behavior, just as Kami-sama had taught them.

5

Kami-sama was the god who had created every-
thing. The people and the animals, the mountains
and the trees, even the four beautiful seasons – all
were created by Kami-sama.

Kami-sama lived in a beautiful palace high up in the sky. From his palace, he was able to watch over his creation below. From sunrise to sunset, he looked after the people and the animals.

Kami-sama granted babies to old couples who had
no children, and he sent furious rains when there was
injustice. He also rewarded hard-working farmers
with lots of golden sunshine.

8

So much was there for Kami-sama to do that he
became very weary.

"I need some help in looking after my creation,"
he said.

He decided to turn to the good animals for help. Dipping his brush in the Milky Way, Kami-sama scribbled a message with ink so bright it glittered like the stars. Kami-sama then sent this message to all the animals.

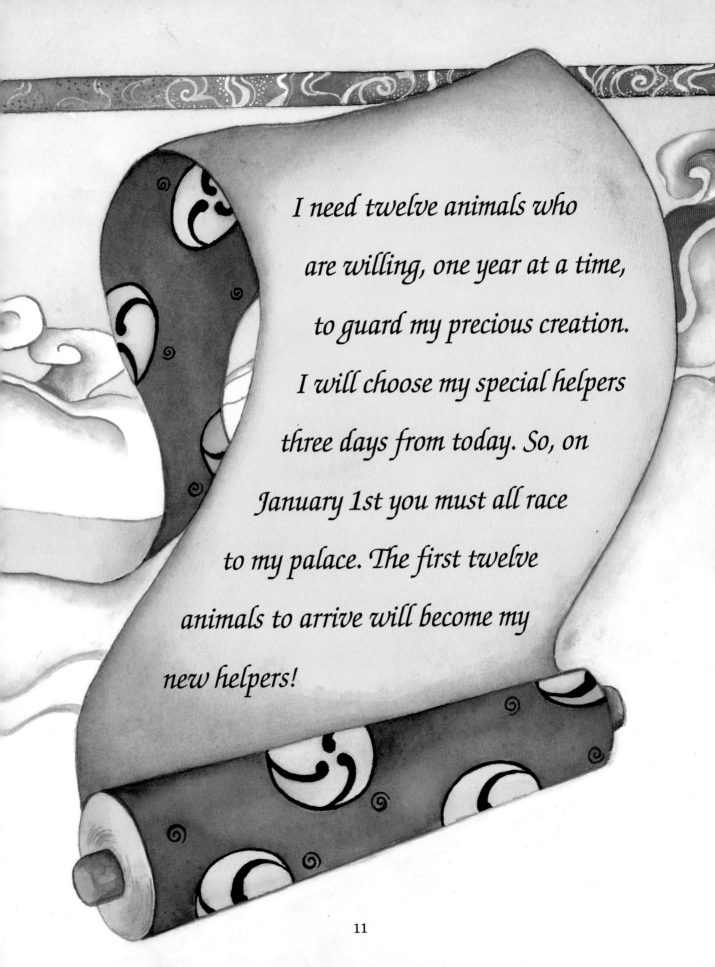

I need twelve animals who are willing, one year at a time, to guard my precious creation. I will choose my special helpers three days from today. So, on January 1st you must all race to my palace. The first twelve animals to arrive will become my new helpers!

As soon as they saw Kami-sama's message, the animals became very excited. This would be a wonderful way to please and serve their beloved Kami-sama. Many animals began to brag about their speed and strength.

12

The only animal who remained silent was Neko-san, the cat. You see, the cat was a lazy creature, and despite all the hustle and bustle, he had curled up into a fluffy ball and had fallen sound asleep!

When Neko-san awoke, the sun was slowly setting behind the nearby mountains. The cat looked around and saw that all of the animals had gone.

"Oh my – has the race begun?" he said to himself. "Was it today?" The dazed cat tried as hard as he could to recall Kami-sama's message but he simply could not remember. Just then, Nezumi-san, the mouse, scurried by.

"Thank goodness, Nezumi-san!" exclaimed the cat. "You have come just in time to answer my question! When is Kami-sama's race?"

The mouse – who was a mischievous little fellow – did not answer the cat right away. He knew that the cat could easily beat him in a race to Kami-sama's palace. This thought made him quite jealous.

"Neko-san, Neko-san," squeaked the mouse. "The race will be held on January 2nd, four days from today!"

The cat thanked the mouse gratefully, not realizing that he had been given the wrong date. Meanwhile, the sneaky little mouse sang happily all the way home, "I'm going to beat Neko-san, yippie, yippie, yay!"

The mouse's home was in the attic of a barn. Also
in this barn lived Ushi-san, the ox. When Nezumi-san
reached the barn, he found the ox with a big bundle
tied to his back.

"Excuse me, Ushi-san," called out the mouse. "Where are you going?"

"I'm leaving early for Kami-sama's palace," replied the ox. "You know how slow I am. Unless I leave tonight, I'll never make it to the palace by January 1st."

When he heard this, the mouse came up with a cunning plan.

"Hmmm... I'm so tiny that I can hide on Ushi-san's back! He'll never notice me, and I'll get a free ride to the palace!"

The slow ox seemed to trudge along forever, his heavy body swaying gently from side to side. Even on the icy mountain path, the ox did not stop.

Ushi-san struggled up the steep path, scrambling from one jagged rock to another. Up and up toward the sky he climbed, snorting and breathing deeply with every step.

Finally, after three nights and two days of endless walking, the ox arrived at Kami-sama's palace. He rejoiced to see that he was the first one to arrive, and he proudly proceeded down the Grand Hallway to the foot of the Heavenly Staircase.

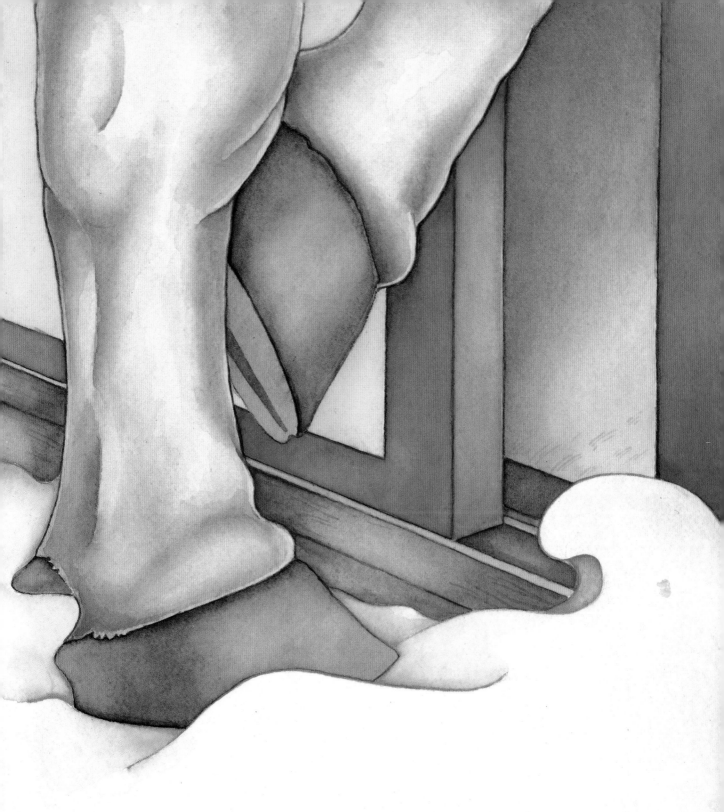

"This must be Kami-sama's chamber!" said the ox,
as he reached the top of the staircase.
Just as he was about to enter through the door...

out jumped Nezumi-san from the bundle on his back. The mouse ran up to Kami-sama and loudly proclaimed, "I am first!" Imagine how surprised the ox was!

Well, the ox was not the only animal to be fooled. The next day, on January 2nd, Neko-san started his journey to Kami-sama's palace at the crack of dawn. Considering how lazy he was, this was a major feat! Neko-san ran as fast as he could to Kami-sama's palace.

As he zigged and zagged through the thick woods, climbed the tallest tree, and pounced from cloud to cloud, Neko-san never once stopped to rest. Finally as he approached the palace gates, he checked to see whether there were any other animals in sight. Seeing no one, he rejoiced.

"Hurrah! I've won!" Neko-san purred happily.

Just as he was about to dart through the palace
gate, a guard stopped him.

"Wait a minute, Neko-san. You're a day late! The
twelve animals were chosen yesterday, on January
1st. Didn't you know that?" asked the guard.

"The mouse got here first," continued the guard.
"Then the ox, the tiger, the rabbit, the dragon, the
snake, the horse, the sheep, the monkey, the rooster,
the dog, and finally the boar. What happened to you?
Were you asleep all day?"

And that's when Neko-san realized the horrifying truth. He had been tricked by Nezumi-san! And even worse – Nezumi-san had arrived at Kami-sama's palace first!

"That sneaky little mouse! I'm never going to let him get away with this!" hissed the cat.

The Guard chuckled.

"It's no use getting angry now. It's all been decided," he said. "Go wash your face and forget about it."

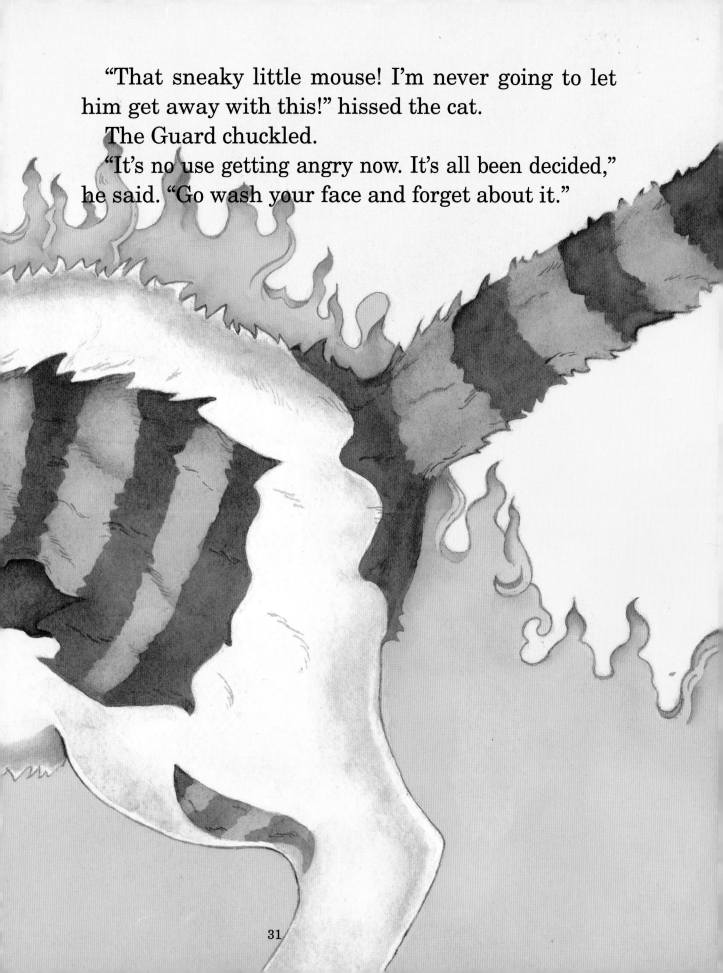

Since that day, cats have chased mice fiercely. The twelve animals chosen by Kami-sama came to be known as the Twelve Signs of the Zodiac. Neko-san, the cat, certainly was not one of them.

That's not all.

Have you ever noticed how often cats wash their faces with their paws? That is because they hear the guard's voice echoing: "Go wash your face and forget about it."